SMELLY BILL

LOVE STINKS

Daniel
Postgate

Albert Whitman & Company
Chicago, Illinois

When Bill saw Peachy Snugglekins
Come trotting past the rubbish bins,
His knees went weak, his eyes grew wide,
He felt all gooey deep inside.

He dropped his bag
of rotting stuff,
He'd seen enough,

He was in love.

He found a rose and snatched it up
Then ran to catch the lucky pup.
But when he saw who clutched her lead,
His world turned very dim, indeed...

The face of Great Aunt Bleach stared down,
With curling lip and hateful frown.

"Get lost!"
she hollered.
"Go on,
shoo!

My Peach is far
too good for you!"

They marched straight past,
snouts in the air,
As if Bill simply wasn't there.

That night Bill couldn't sleep. Instead
He climbed onto the garden shed

OOOO

OOOOAAAAWWWOOO

And howled and yowled up at the moon
A loud and melancholy tune,
About the love he couldn't win
Because Peach was too good for him.

Next day, Bill's folks woke up to see
Something quite extraordinary:
Their stinking pet sat in the tub...

Begging for a soapy scrub!

Now later in the park that day,
A "dog parade" got underway.
The poshest dogs you'll ever see,
The finest in their pedigree,
Had come in every shape and size
To try and win the
"Best Dog" prize.

Peach was also at the show
Splendid in her scarlet bow,
But who was that among the crowd,
Looking like an orange cloud
With crooked snout and snaggled teeth;
And very skinny legs
      beneath?

What creature was it, can you tell?

Why, it was Bill without the smell!
He'd come to prove he was as fine
As any fancy-pants canine.

The chatting crowd began to hush.
"He's like a walking
toilet brush!"
Some rather nasty person sneered.

And while the others laughed and jeered,
Bill turned around and, in dismay,
He slowly, sadly, slunk away.

Just then the show was interrupted
When Vesuvius erupted.
Vesuvius, a giant hound,
Chased all the other
dogs around!

Then roaring, growling, **barking, snarling**
Went for Great Aunt Bleach's darling!

Poor Peach shot off across the park.
She dashed into a forest, dark;
Hoping that he wouldn't find her,
But the beast was right behind her!

Into a boggy swamp she flew
And promptly sank into
the goo.

"Please save my
    Peachy-kins!" Bleach cried
         When all the other
              folk arrived.

But they just snorted,
"No chance, ducky,
We don't want our clothing mucky."
Bleach howled and screamed,
she begged and wept...

Then suddenly a creature leapt
And sploshed into that filthy bog
To save Aunt Bleach's precious dog.

Which
creature
was it,
can you tell?

Of course,
it was our
Smelly Bill!

Bleach hugged Bill to her grateful chest.
"I think we know which dog's the best...
Bill stinks, but he is brave and bold
And has a heart of solid gold!"

Then Bleach said
something very strange:

She whispered,
"Bill, please never change."

Later, when the day was done,
Our hero watched the evening sun
Turn slowly to a shade of red
And sink behind the garden shed.

He sat with his new sweetheart, Peach,
Who he'd so bravely saved...

To all at
Whitstable Endowed
Junior School

The CIP record is available from the Library of Congress.

Text and illustrations copyright © 2009 Daniel Postgate.
First published in Great Britain by Meadowside Children's Books.
Published in 2010 by Albert Whitman & Company.
ISBN 978-0-8075-7464-5
Printed in China.
10 9 8 7 6 5 4 3 2 1 BP 15 14 13 12 11 10

For more information about Albert Whitman & Company,
please visit our web site at www.albertwhitman.com.